THE URBANA FREE LIBRARY

W9-BBQ-275

DATE DUE

DISCARDED BY THE
URBANA FREE LIBRARY

The Urbana Free Library

To renew: call 217-367-4057
or go to "*urbanafreelibrary.org*"
and select "Renew/Request Items"

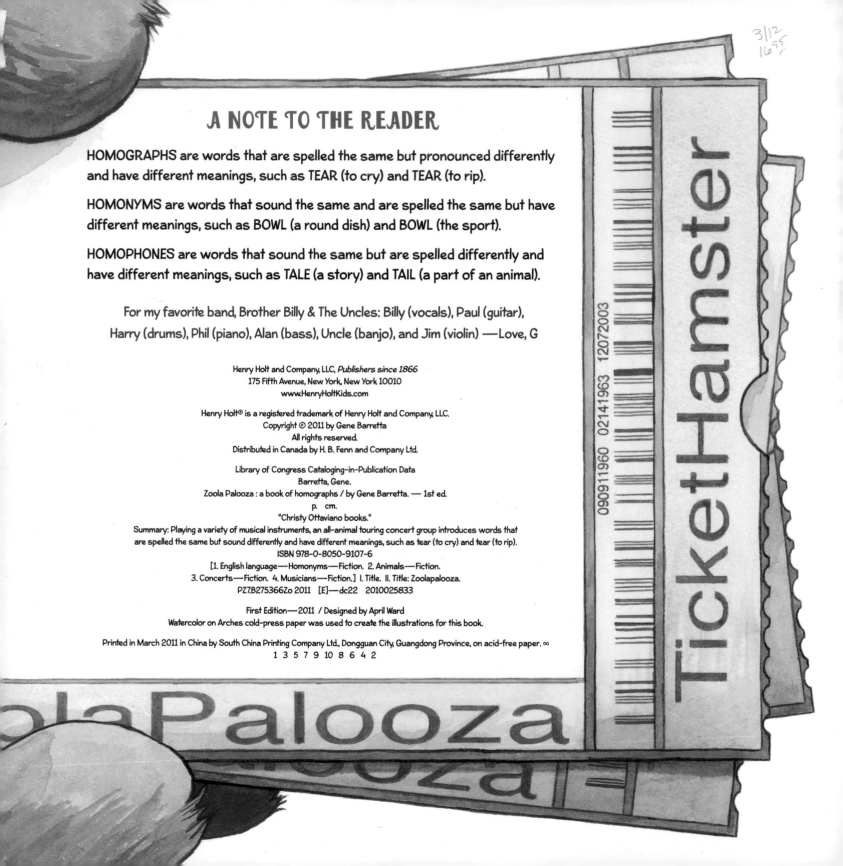

A NOTE TO THE READER

HOMOGRAPHS are words that are spelled the same but pronounced differently and have different meanings, such as TEAR (to cry) and TEAR (to rip).

HOMONYMS are words that sound the same and are spelled the same but have different meanings, such as BOWL (a round dish) and BOWL (the sport).

HOMOPHONES are words that sound the same but are spelled differently and have different meanings, such as TALE (a story) and TAIL (a part of an animal).

For my favorite band, Brother Billy & The Uncles: Billy (vocals), Paul (guitar), Harry (drums), Phil (piano), Alan (bass), Uncle (banjo), and Jim (violin) —Love, G

Henry Holt and Company, LLC, *Publishers since 1866*
175 Fifth Avenue, New York, New York 10010
www.HenryHoltKids.com

Henry Holt® is a registered trademark of Henry Holt and Company, LLC.
Copyright © 2011 by Gene Barretta
All rights reserved.
Distributed in Canada by H. B. Fenn and Company Ltd.

Library of Congress Cataloging-in-Publication Data
Barretta, Gene.
Zoola Palooza : a book of homographs / by Gene Barretta. — 1st ed.
p. cm.
"Christy Ottaviano books."
Summary: Playing a variety of musical instruments, an all-animal touring concert group introduces words that
are spelled the same but sound differently and have different meanings, such as tear (to cry) and tear (to rip).
ISBN 978-0-8050-9107-6
[1. English language—Homonyms—Fiction. 2. Animals—Fiction.
3. Concerts—Fiction. 4. Musicians—Fiction.] I. Title. II. Title: Zoolapalooza.
PZ7.B275366Zo 2011 [E]—dc22 2010025833

First Edition—2011 / Designed by April Ward
Watercolor on Arches cold-press paper was used to create the illustrations for this book.

Printed in March 2011 in China by South China Printing Company Ltd., Dongguan City, Guangdong Province, on acid-free paper. ∞
1 3 5 7 9 10 8 6 4 2

ZOOLA PALOOZA

A Book of Homographs

Gene
Barretta

Christy Ottaviano Books

Henry Holt and Company

NEW YORK

ENTRANCE
and
~~CRICKETS~~
TICKETS

Have you READ about the greatest concert
in the animal kingdom?
We just saw it! READ my shirt—
"Zoola Palooza. No cages. Just stages."

Billy the striped **BASS** opened the show
wearing a big striped **BOW** tie.
He took a gracious **BOW** from the top
of his **BASS** fiddle.

Carter Piller was on stage NUMBER two.

He played a 30-MINUTE solo with a guitar

that was so loud and yet so MINUTE.

His fingers were numb—

but our ears were NUMBER.

The drummer for The Catnip Clan was exhausted.

Usually that cat lives to REBEL.

But today he was just

a REBEL without his claws.

Carmen Chameleon's ENTRANCE
will ENTRANCE you.
She's the only singer we know
who can PRODUCE a fresh bowl
of PRODUCE and blend into it.

The Seagull Sisters PRESENT

their songs high above the stage.

Don't be surprised if they

drop you a PRESENT.

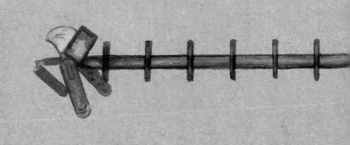

There will be no official
RECORD of the show.
The sound engineers forgot
to press the RECORD button.

The scariest moment was when
Sally Mander dressed up like a **DOVE**
and **DOVE** into the audience.
Fortunately, she **WOUND** up landing
on the back of a jellyfish, **WOUND**-free.

They had to CONSOLE the worried stage crew after the power CONSOLE blew up. But the light show was amazing!

Florence Welk had a fresh coat of POLISH
on her POLKA-dot accordion.

As soon as she played it, everyone danced
the POLKA and waved the POLISH flag.

The Crying Crocodiles gave
TEAR-stained towels to everyone.
We're going to TEAR ours into pieces
and make more Croco-Dolls.

DOES The Dear Deer Band have
the PERFECT fan club?

Yes! They call themselves The Fa-So-La-Te-DOES
and spend hours trying to PERFECT their antlers.

The crowd was pretty rowdy at The Rabbits show.

Fluff Daddy stopped and shouted,

"EXCUSE me. There's no EXCUSE for that!

Do I have to SEPARATE you guys

and give you each a SEPARATE time-out?"

Hedda Hip-Hopper was a prime
SUSPECT in today's big scandal.
We SUSPECT someone else
was doing her singing.

Seals & Crawfish always CLOSE the concert
the same way. They WIND up their Victrola and
blow crawfish out of their WIND instruments.
If you're hungry, sit up CLOSE.

So there's no USE hanging around. We'll USE
these tickets and follow the show from town to town.
We'll LIVE in our car and get Daddy to drive.
Because nothing beats seeing . . .